Mrs. Popish's PICKLES

Written by Tiffany Haifley

Illustrated by Rachel Oldfield

To Kathy~
I hope you laugh when you read about Mrs. Popish's adventures!
Tiff

To all my people who came alongside me
on this journey— I'm forever grateful.

T.H.

For my Dad, thank you for inspiring me.

R.O

Published by Orange Hat Publishing 2024
PB ISBN: 9781645387343
HC ISBN: 9781645387336

Copyrighted © 2024 by Tiffany Haifley
All Rights Reserved
Mrs. Popish's Pickles
Written by Tiffany Haifley
Illustrated by Rachel Oldfield

This publication and all contents within may not be reproduced or transmitted in any part or in its entirety without the written permission of the author.

orangehatpublishing.com

Mr. Popish *loves* pickles.
He's truly obsessed.
He eats them all day;
he wants only the best!

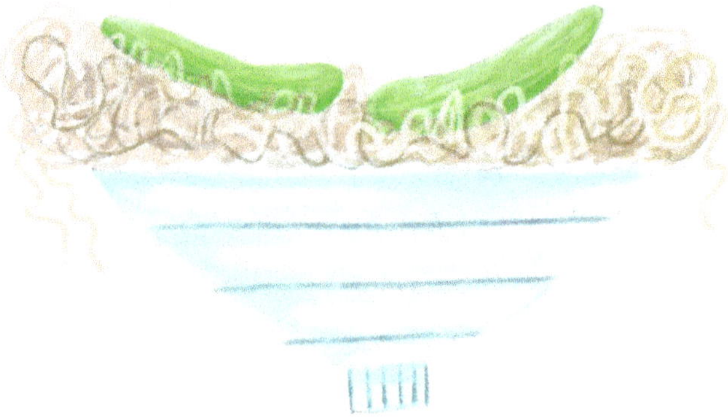

He eats them for breakfast and loves them for lunch.

He always ends dinner by sneaking a crunch.

His wife makes his favorite.
Her recipe's best. Thanksgiving? Christmas? They're his only request!

She plants them each spring. But upon his review, there won't be enough . . . So he plants some too!

Cucumbers here, cucumbers there.
Cucumbers, cucumbers everywhere!

They're sprouting and spreading and sprawling like mad.
They're climbing and vining; it's really quite bad!

They must pick them and pickle them, all in one day.
Because waiting too long makes the crunch go away.

But how will they wash them?
Just what will they do?
They must think of something
before the day's through.

Cucumbers here, cucumbers there.
Cucumbers, cucumbers everywhere!

Into the sink,
it won't do the trick.
Too many to wash,
they need something quick!

Into the tub.
The cukes overflow!
But—*oof!* As they scrub,
they can't bend that low!

They load up the truck to clear the debris.

Off to the carwash . . .

Cucumbers here, cucumbers there. Cucumbers, cucumbers

Just how will they wash them? What could they try next?

She knows what to do! What could be more routine?

She runs load after load...

They pick and pickle, they can, and they jar.
He places a peck in the back of their car . . .
He's packed her a suitcase for a pickle contest.

He's entered her recipe. He knows it's the best!

Sweet ones and dill ones— oh, where to begin?

After tasting them all, he knows she will win.

Mary A. Popish

was a real person who actually washed her cucumbers in the washing machine! She lived in Denver from the 1920s to the 1980s, grew a fruitful garden, loved bingo, had four children, and cared for the priests at her local parish. She had an amazing pickle recipe that she shared with Uncle Virgil who loved pickles. He followed her recipe to the letter—including picking and pickling all in one day, using the washing machine to get the cukes washed in time, and never opening the jars before they were ready. His son lived on the East Coast, and together they entered and won a contest. Virgil was an enthusiastic storyteller, and I always imagined him traveling around in a giant pickle-mobile (like the Oscar Meyer Weinermobile) from Denver to the East Coast, attending and winning contests, and eating countless pickles along the way.

Sis, Mom, me, Frank
John.

MRS. POPISH'S DILL-ICIOUS PICKLES
(makes 24 quart jars)

Ingredients/Supplies:

- ½ bushel (about 250) FRESH PICKED 3-4" pickling cucumbers, rinsed in sink, then washed in the washing machine*
- 3 big bunches of fresh dill (size of broccoli heads)
- 10 jalapeño peppers about 4" long (cut in 2-3 pieces)
- 1 gallon apple cider vinegar, 5% acidity**
- 3 pounds pickling salt or coarse kosher salt
- 1 large bulb garlic (cut the cloves into 2-3 pieces)
- 24 wide-mouth quart canning jars
- Canning lids and rings

In each wide-mouth quart jar add:
- 1 large sprig of dill plus 3 small sprigs
- 1 clove of garlic cut into 3 pieces
- Only 2 pieces of jalapeño! (including seeds)
- 10-12 cucumbers, leaving ½-inch room at top of jar

Make the brine (enough for 6 jars at a time)
- Bring 3 quarts water and 1 quart vinegar to a rolling boil.
- Add 1 cup pickling or kosher salt (slowly, or you'll have a volcano!).
- Pour brine into jars making sure all cucumbers are covered (Leave ½ inch open at the top).

SEALING THE JARS

1. Boil rings only and turn off the heat.

2. Put lids in a separate pan, pour some of the hot water from the rings over them. Do not boil lids.

3. Wipe jar rims.

4. Put lids on jars and screw rings on as tight as possible.

5. At this point, you could be an official canner/preserver and water-bath the jars. This is the official recommendation from the food science people so you don't get listeria—look at us learning about microbiology! If you'd like to live on the edge like our family, continue with Mrs. Popish's instructions.

6. After sealing about half of the jars, turn them upside down on the table.

7. Finish sealing the rest and flip them upside down.

8. Turn the first jars right side up, then wait a few minutes and turn the next set. Lids should begin to ping as they cool.

9. Store in a cool, dry place and DO NOT OPEN for 3 months. This will be a good test of your willpower and self-control. No sneaking a sample before they're ready!

*How clean is your washing machine? Have your brother's dirty socks and practice uniforms been fermenting in there? While pickling is similar to fermenting, WE ARE NOT TRYING TO BOTTLE THAT. Maybe just use the sink.

**Make at your own risk—you might get botulism! Look at us learning more about microbiology! Keep your pickles safe by using the correct acidity. Also, don't eat anything that smells bad, even if your older brother dares you or offers you lots of money.

VERY IMPORTANT: NEVER make pickles without an adult, preferably one who loves pickles as much as you.

Have I scared your adult with all this botulism and listeria talk? If so, visit your local university's extension office for more information on food preservation, or visit tiffanyhaifley.com to find out more.

Printed in the USA
CPSIA information can be obtained
at www.ICGtesting.com
LVHW060042010524
778942LV00003B/7

9 781645 387336